The   oys

A & C BLACK • LONDON

Contents

A Letter from the Playwright

In 1982 I received a phone call from the head of the London Primary where my sons were at school. A parent-composer had offered to compose an original musical for the school but didn't write *words*. They knew I wrote children's books. Would I give it a shot? The result was what I call the 'Mavis Musicals,' after the late Mavis Gotto, inspired teacher and stager each year of the school play.

Mavis had a stubborn attachment to the potential excellence of every child she taught and an uncanny instinct for latent talent and her productions were designed to help realise it. It is with her voice constantly in my head that I have written *The Good-Time Boys* with, I hope, parts for everyone from the natural actors and innately musical through the comics and show-offs to the shy and less confident.

The play itself, based on a folktale, is set in East Africa around the turn of this century. I have inevitably modernised and westernised the language but the basic style remains African in that here the company of actors *is the play*, just as the play requires — the grass, the trees, the walls of the house, the lake lapping, the wind blowing — as well as the so-called main parts.

One advantage of this style is that since the actors are everything, there is little call for scenery. Another is that everyone works together, sometimes playing more than one role, with the result that all the parts are equally valuable to the dramatic effectiveness of the whole.

At the end of the day, however, and in memory of Mavis, all I hope is that everyone involved in whatever level of production, can suspend disbelief for its duration, evoke another world — *Africa* — and with much stamping, drumming, chanting, emotion and energy, have a rewarding experience along the way.

A note on pronunciation

The African names in the script are easily pronounced: slide consonants and vowels together exactly as they're written.

Ajidi	Ah-jee-dee
Amini	Ah-mee-nee
Njobvu	En-*joh*-b'voo
Tsekewe	*Tsay*-kway
Nomvula	Nom-*voo*-lah
Kapok	*Kay*-pok

Characters In Order Of Appearance

Trees (2–4)
The Kapok Tree
Walls of the House (2–4)
Ajidi
Amini
Mamma Nomvula
Two Swallows
Two Storks
Bushcat
Lemur
Osprey
Four Uncles
Four Village Elders
Villagers (any number)

Tsekwe the Goose
Mrs Tsekwe his wife
The Wind (at least 4)
Njobvu the Elephant
Thorn Bushes (2–4)
The Bridge Rails (at least 6)
Long Grass (2–4)
Rushes (2–4)
The River (at least 4)
Whipper-Snapper, the Ant
Lapping Water (2–4)
The Army of White Ants

Two drummers

List of Scenes and their Locations

Act 1

Scene 1 — The Debt   In the Village
Scene 2 — As Good as Paid   Out in the Bush
Scene 3 — Over to the Geese   At the Edge of a Lake
Scene 4 — Natural Disaster   Around the Kapok Tree

(Interval if desired)

Act 2

Scene 1 — Over to Kapok   Around the Kapok Tree
Scene 2 — Over to Elephant   Around the Kapok Tree
Scene 3 — Over to the Ants   At the Bridge
Scene 4 — All is Lost   In and around the Anthill
Scene 5 — Wisdom Came Too   In the Village

Act 1, Scene 1 — The Debt

In the Village. THE DRUMMERS, (seated and on stage throughout) start a soft rhythmic drumming. THE TREES and THE WALLS OF THE HOUSE enter and arrange themselves. MAMMA NOMVULA is inside the house unseen by the audience. AJIDI and AMINI enter from opposite sides of the stage. They slap hands in greeting.

MAMMA NOMVULA: *(wailing from inside THE WALLS OF THE HOUSE)*
Aaai, aaai, aaai!

(THE WALLS put their hands behind their ears to listen. THE UNCLES entering, stop and listen. THE WALLS part to make a door.)

MAMMA NOMVULA: Aaaai! Aaaai! *(She appears at the door.)* Wild boys! Wild boys! My sons are wild boys. They think of nothing but a good time.

THE UNCLES: Wild boys! Wild boys! Her sons are wild boys. They think of nothing but a good time.

THE WALLS: Nothing but a good time.

(THE DRUMMERS beat out the rhythm 'Nothing but a good time' as AMINI and AJIDI sit on the ground and play dice with bones. The drumming stops.)

MAMMA NOMVULA: I am a good woman.

UNCLES: You are, sister.

MAMMA NOMVULA: Then tell me, Uncles, what did I do to get sons like these? Aaai, aaai, aaai!

FIRST UNCLE: These young men grew up in our village.

SECOND UNCLE: We are all responsible for their ways.

THIRD UNCLE: Then we must not be afraid to act.

FOURTH UNCLE: Come, let us call a council with the Elders.

(THE UNCLES exit. THE DRUMMERS beat the rhythm 'Call a council with the Elders' as the TREES and WALLS chant.)

TREES and WALLS: *(chanting)* Call a council with the Elders. Call a council with the Elders.

(THE ELDERS and UNCLES enter. THE ELDERS sit under the trees.)

FIRST DRUMMER: The Council of Elders is called.

SECOND DRUMMER: The Elders are wise.

FIRST and
SECOND TREES: They have been here a long time.

THIRD and
FOURTH TREES: They have seen today before.

THE WALLS: They will know what to do about the wild boys. They will know.

FIRST ELDER: Let the brothers come before us.

FIRST UNCLE: Call the brothers. Call the whole village.

(THE DRUMMERS drum the rhythm 'Call the brothers'. THE VILLAGERS enter. AMINI and AJIDI hide their dice and approach THE ELDERS.)

SECOND ELDER: Amini and Ajidi, sons of Mamma Nomvula, it has come to our notice that when there is work to be done, you are never to be found doing it. So, tell us in your own words, what do you do with your days?

AMINI: Uh... we hunt, Honoured One.

AJIDI: And fish, Your Wisdom. And sing...

AMINI: And dance, Your Greatness...

AJIDI: And lay traps for lizards and rob hives for honey...

AMINI:	And confuse the chameleon. And swim in the deep pool at the gorge...
AJIDI:	And admire the leopard's spots.
AMINI:	And race the hare...
AJIDI:	Or race each other!
AMINI:	Or lie in the shade and watch the clouds.
AJIDI:	Or hide in the trees and watch the girls...
MAMMA NOMVULA:	*(wailing)* Aaai, aaai, aaai!
SECOND ELDER:	Amini and Ajidi, you have answered truthfully. Now answer something else. While you are out enjoying yourselves, what do you think the rest of the village is doing?
AMINI and AJIDI:	*(shuffle sheepishly)* Uh... the same?
THIRD ELDER:	Wrong. While you are chasing a good time, your mother and uncles and sisters and aunts and brothers and cousins and neighbours are hard at it...

(THE VILLAGERS, UNCLES and MAMMA NOMVULA begin to stamp their feet rhythmically as they chant the following song.)

Sowing and hoeing and tending and bending,
Reaping and threshing and weeding and seeding,
Sweeping and cooking and stirring the stew,
Chopping and hewing and looking for YOU!

FOURTH ELDER:	Amini and Ajidi, listen and listen well. Life in this village is like the stew the women stir.
THIRD ELDER:	Everyone puts something into the pot.
SECOND ELDER:	Except for you. You only take from the pot.

THE VILLAGERS: (*muttering amongst themselves*) It's true.

FIRST ELDER: So it is decided. You will leave and not return until you have learned how to live useful lives and can repay your — <u>debt</u>!

MAMMA NOMVULA: Oh my children! Oh my sons! Sent away forever!

(*AMINI and AJIDI each fall to one knee.*)

AJIDI: Very well, Fathers, if it is decided, we will go. All we ask is a hoe and an axe and a bag of seed.

FIRST ELDER: We will see what can be done about the matter.

(*The VILLAGERS gather to sing or chant and watch AMINI & AJIDI preparing to leave. An UNCLE hands AMINI an axe. Another UNCLE hands AJIDI a hoe and an ELDER gives him a bag of seed. THE VILLAGERS sing or chant the following song.*)

<u>A HOE, AN AXE, A BAG OF SEED</u>

A hoe, an axe and a bag of seed
Are all the wild boys think they need
To start a life out on their own
Away from what they've loved and known

(*THE TREES, WALLS, ELDERS, UNCLES and MAMMA NOMVULA join in.*)

But time will teach and they'll soon see
It also takes some in...dus...try...
Little bit of work and a little bit of sweat
Little bit of what they've not done yet

But time will teach and they'll soon see
It also takes some in...dus...try...
Little bit of work and a little bit of sweat
Little bit of what they've not done yet!

UNCLES
and ELDERS: (*speaking over the singing*) Haai! These good-time boys. They don't even know which end of the hoe to hold!

A hoe, an axe and a bag of seed
Are all the wild boys think they'll need
To get a field of rice to grow
And pay the village what they owe...

(AMINI and AJIDI trudge off and all exit singing.)

But time will teach and they'll soon see...
It also takes some in...dus...try
Little bit of work and a little bit of sweat
Little bit of what they've not done yet!

Act 1, Scene 2 — As Good as Paid

Out in the Bush. THE TREES, THORN BUSHES and LONG GRASS enter and arrange themselves. THE GRASS rustles and whispers. We hear the sounds of birds and cicadas from off stage. AMINI and AJIDI enter, walking in single file.

AMINI: *(playing with the word)* Debt, debt, debt? <u>Debt</u>? De...Eh...Tt. DEBT?

AJIDI: Oh stop it, Amini. It's all I've heard for miles.

AMINI: But it's such a strange word. Debt? Tell me again, what is a <u>debt</u>?

(AJIDI stops and leans on the hoe.)

AJIDI: For the last time, Amini, a debt is something you <u>owe</u>. Something you have to <u>give back</u>. In our case this rice we're going to have to <u>grow</u>, to <u>give back</u>, so we can <u>go back</u>. Now come on, try and keep up!

AMINI: I'm too tired. I can't go on. And I'm starving...

(There is loud honking of geese from off stage.)

AMINI: *(lifting his bow and arrow)* Oh, what I'd give for one of those fat geese up there, baked in clay, the way the women do it back home.

LONG GRASS: *(whispering)* It'll be a long time before he tastes that again!

(AJIDI is staring out into the audience.)

AJIDI: Forget about your hunger for five swats at a fly, Amini, and come and look at this!

AMINI: By all the spirits of our ancestors! It's a lake... a great, shining, blue lake! We've discovered a lake!

TREES, BUSHES,
GRASS: *(whispering)* No, it's always been there...

AJIDI: A great shining lake with long, wet, marshy shores. Just made for growing this. *(He waves the bag of seed.)* There in front of us, a waving field of green and golden rice. Brother, don't you see? Our debt is as good as paid!

(AMINI snatches the bag of rice from AJIDI.)

AMINI: Except for one thing, Ajidi. The rice is in here, not there.

AJIDI: Then we must waste no time. You start by clearing the ground.

AMINI: What?

AJIDI: You have the axe, don't you?

AMINI: And what'll you be doing?

AJIDI: Planning.

AMINI: You mean dreaming.

AJIDI: Someone has to have the vision.

(THE DRUMMERS drum the axe rhythm. THE TREES, BUSHES AND GRASS gather together and mime chopping and clearing. AMINI leads the actions while AJIDI, leaning on the hoe, looks on. AMINI and THE TREES, BUSHES and GRASS chant the following verse.)

Up, down, hack and hew
Chop it, chop it, cut it through
Where tangled reeds and roots are found
Hack, hew to clear the ground!
Hack, hew to clear the ground!
Hack, hew and keep it going
Hack, hew...

AJIDI: ... and now the hoeing!

(AJIDI hands AMINI the hoe. THE TREES, BUSHES and GRASS regroup and
mime hoeing the ground. A weary AMINI leads the actions while AJIDI takes a nap.
AMINI and THE TREES, BUSHES and GRASS chant the next verse.)

Push, pull, lift and break
Back, forward, sift and rake
If tender shoots will ever grow
Push, pull, and work the hoe
Push, pull, and work the hoe
Push, pull and on we go
Push, pull...

AJIDI: (leaping up) ... and now I'll sow!

(THE TREES, BUSHES AND GRASS resume being trees, bushes and grass.
AMINI collapses, exhausted.)

AJIDI: (miming scattering seed) Well, brother Amini, together, we've
                         done it. From the wild, marshy shores of a lost lake we have
                         created a rice field. Not bad, for two good-time boys, huh?

AMINI: Not quite the same as lying in the shade seeing shapes
                         in the clouds...

AJIDI: (shaking out the empty seed bag) But maybe more
                         satisfying. I could even take to this work thing.

AMINI: And I may take to dreaming. Now, can we eat?

AJIDI: Good idea. We'll go back to that cave we found and cook
                         up a big muula fruit stew.

AMINI: *(picking up the axe and hoe)* Only jackals eat muula fruit, Ajidi.

(There is a honking of geese from off stage.)

AMINI: *(gazing up into the sky)* And those geese are getting closer...

AJIDI: Fine by me. You choose the menu.

(They exit — AJIDI, striding ahead, AMINI carrying the tools and clutching his aching back. THE TREES, BUSHES and GRASS exit. THE DRUMMERS create a 'husha husha' sound.)

Act 1, Scene 3 — Over To The Geese

At the edge of a lake. THE RUSHES and LAKE WATER enter and arrange themselves. The RUSHES sway slightly. THE WATER, using their cloaks, make lapping movements.

RUSHES
AND WATER: *(murmuring)* Sshhlap, sshhlap... slish, slish...sshhlap, sshhlap...

(TSEKWE and MRS TSEKWE enter. They waddle across the stage, looking around curiously. THE DRUMMERS stop making the 'husha husha' sound.)

MRS TSEKWE: Oh, good husband, Tsekwe. Do you see what I see?

TSEKWE: *(teasing)* You know I am only permitted to see what you tell me I see. So tell me what you see and I am sure that will be what I see.

MRS TSEKWE: Don't tease me, Tsekwe. Not now. Not today, when I'm sooooo empty here. *(She rubs her tum)*... home of my good moods. Just take a look and tell me if you are seeing what I am seeing.

TSEKWE: Well, my dear, I am certainly seeing freshly-turned earth. And one thing we both know is, where there's freshly-turned earth, there's always...

TSEKWE AND
MRS TSEKWE: Se-e-e-e-d!

(THE TSEKWES mime eating rice seed, stretching out their necks and pecking at the ground. THE DRUMMERS start to drum a rhythm. Then the RUSHES and WATER sing or chant the following song.)

A HOE, AN AXE, A BAG OF SEED (reprise)

A hoe, an axe and a bag of seed
Were all the wild boys thought they'd need
Together with some toil and sweat
To grow their rice and pay their debt
But now they'll see their hopes decrease
They had not planned on HUN... GRY... GEESE!

(AJIDI and AMINI tiptoe in. AJIDI has a finger to his lips.)

AMINI: *(in a stage whisper)* I tell you, Ajidi, there'll be nothing to see. Rice just does not grow that quickly. And it certainly can't hear footsteps.

AJIDI: How do you know? You've never been near a rice field. Let alone a growing one.

AMINI: Nor have you.

(AJIDI spots the GEESE and dances with rage. AMINI puts an arrow in his bow and aims at MRS TSEKWE.)

AJIDI: Hey! Oi! You! Shoo! Off! What d'you think you're doing? That's our rice!

AMINI: Forget rice! *(He pulls his bow string back.)* Forget muula stew. It is goose for dinner tonight!

(TSEKWE does a crazed dance, throwing himself at AMINI'S feet.)

TSEKWE: I beg you, Honoured Wingless Boy, do not let your arrow fly. That beautiful creature is my wife.

AMINI: *(hesitating)* Sorry?

TSEKWE: My beautiful wife whom I love and with whom I hope soon to have a large family.

(AMINI squints at AJIDI. He can't believe what he's hearing. AJIDI is taken aback too.)

AJIDI: What do we care? You've just eaten the rice we were growing...

AMINI: *(Re-aiming at Mrs TSEKWE.)*... so we can return to our village and pay our <u>debt</u>!

TSEKWE: Wait! If we've eaten your only means of paying a debt and you forgive us...

AMINI: ... then what, goose?

TSEKWE: ... the debt passes to us! <u>We owe you</u>!

MRS TSEKWE: *(raising her head)* He's right, you know. *(To TSEKWE)* Now I know why I married you, you're so clever. *(To the BOYS)* Would a flock of ten healthy goslings go any way towards paying this debt?

AJIDI: Ten healthy goslings!

AMINI: Which would grow into ten healthy geese!

AJIDI: All laying lots of healthy eggs. Why, that would more than do it!

AMINI: *(putting the arrow back in his quiver)* Muula fruit stew it certainly is then.

(MRS TSEKWE gets up. TSEKWE puts a protective wing around her.)

TSEKWE:	Our nest is over the hill beneath the Kapok Tree.
MRS TSEKWE:	Come and see us there in the time it takes. *(To TSEKWE)* Now, we have things to do.

(Lovingly, the GEESE waddle off. AMINI, AJIDI and THE RUSHES exit. THE LAPPING WATER rises and runs off stage.)

Act 1, Scene 4 — Natural Disaster

Around the Kapok Tree. The KAPOK TREE takes up her position centre stage. THE BUSHCAT, LEMUR and OSPREY enter. THE TSEKWES proudly place their nest beneath the KAPOK TREE and MRS TSEKWE plumps down on it. MR and MRS STORK and SWALLOW enter and 'perch' around the tree. THE WIND whirls in, rushing across the stage and off again.

TSEKWE:	That was a strong wind for the time of year. Are you all right, my dear?
MRS TSEKWE:	*(smoothing her ruffled feathers)* I'm fine, husband, thank you!
MR STORK:	And the eggs with which you are going to pay your debt to the Wingless Boys?
MRS TSEKWE:	All present and correct, thank you, Mr Stork. Though I am worried about you, Kapok Tree. You were creaking rather loudly.
KAPOK TREE:	Never. Not me.
MR STORK:	I hate to say it, but Mrs Tsekwe's right. Some of your branches aren't at all safe.
MRS STORK:	That's because you're too generous, Kapok Tree. You let everyone, but <u>everyone</u>, sit on you...
KAPOK TREE:	*(flamboyantly)* Well, you know how it is. I just can't resist the company...

(THE KAPOK TREE sings or recites the following song:)

EVERYONE IS WELCOME

Everyone is welcome, every bird and bee
Everyone who wants to — can come and nest in me
Everyone is welcome, everyone is free
To settle in the branches of the Kapok Tree!

(ALL join in:)
Everyone is welcome, in feathers or in fur
Everyone who wants to — can come and rest on her
Everyone is welcome, everyone is free
To settle in the branches of the Kapok Tree!

Everyone is welcome, swallow, stork and kite
Everyone who needs a place to sleep at night
Everyone is welcome, everyone is free
To come and have a chin-wag in the Kapok Tree...

KAPOK TREE: That's right!

(There is the sound of thunder from off stage. THE DRUMMERS make a threatening drumming noise.)

OSPREY: Storm-alert! Storm-alert!

KAPOK TREE: Don't fuss. That storm's far away.

TSEKWE: But getting closer and closer. Hold on to your branches, Kapok Tree...

(The WIND re-enters. This time its whirling is much stronger and the KAPOK TREE sways dramatically. THE BIRDS tuck their heads down under their wings or legs. THE OSPREY, LEMUR and BUSHCAT look afraid.)

(THE WIND sings or chants the last verse of 'Everyone is Welcome'.)

Everyone is welcome, in feathers or in fur
Everyone who wants to — can come and nest in her
But what she hasn't thought of, what she hasn't seen...
She isn't still a sapling, her branches aren't that green...

ALL: *(interrupting the singing to say)* <u>Creeaaaa....kkk</u>!

(THE WIND continues.)

Nothing's going to save them, nothing holds them back
When Nature says their time is up — it's <u>crack, crack, crack</u>!

(THE KAPOK TREE, 'drops' the big branch above the TSEKWES' nest. MRS TSEKWE leaps to safety. But the branch crashes on to the nest. THE KAPOK TREE and BIRDS shriek. THE WIND whirls off stage.)

MRS TSEKWE: My eggs! My beautiful eggs! My unhatched darlings!
                            All broken, all smashed. Oh husband, how will I bear it?

TSEKWE: *(puts his wing round her, but speaks to the audience)*
                          <u>And how will we now pay our debt</u>?

(ALL turn to the audience and speak in unison.)

ALL: <u>How will they now pay their debt</u>?

(ALL freeze. Lights out. ALL exit, THE TSEKWES taking the nest off stage with them.)

INTERVAL

Act 2, Scene 1 — Over To Kapok

Around the Kapok Tree. THE SWALLOWS, STORKS, OSPREY, BUSHCAT, LEMUR, THE TSEKWES, AMINI and AJIDI are gathered round the KAPOK TREE and the fallen branch.

AMINI:	But this is dreadful!
AJIDI:	A disaster!
KAPOK TREE:	And it's all my fault! I was vain. I wouldn't admit any part of me could age!
MR STORK:	I did warn you...
KAPOK TREE:	You all warned me. I'm not as young as I was and I couldn't face it and now your lovely brood is... no more.

(MRS TSEKWE gives an extra loud sob.)

TSEKWE:	There, there, my dear. It's a disaster, but a natural one. And in time, there will be other eggs, I promise. But right now, Wingless Boys, there are no goslings.
KAPOK TREE :	Ohhh!

(TSEKWE spreads his wings out to expose his breast for AMINI'S arrow and closes his eyes.)

TSEKWE:	And so if you must eat goose, let it be me, not my wife.
AMINI:	I wouldn't hear of it! You have quite enough to deal with!
AJIDI:	*(laying it on thick)* Amini's right. Our rice is gone, the goslings are gone, we'll probably never see our mother again, but...
KAPOK TREE:	Wait! What are we talking about, Boys? If I let a branch fall on the eggs the Tsekwes were going to give you, then it's simple. The debt passes to me! I must give something!

(Everyone murmurs. There is a general hum of 'Ah, yes, hmmm, that makes sense.')

AMINI: That's very kind of you, Kapok, but what — er, apart from your beauty, of course — could you offer us?

KAPOK TREE: When my flowers have finished blooming they turn to cotton. The softest silkiest cotton in the world. You shall have the lot!

AMINI: Ajidi! The women back home can turn cotton into cloth!

AJIDI: Then our debt is paid! It's paid! It's paid!

(AMINI & AJIDI give each other a 'high five'.)

BUSHCAT: And your mother might even get a new head-dress out of all the suffering you've given her.

AMINI: This is most generous, Kapok Tree.

KAPOK TREE: The very least I can do. Come back when it's time and collect!

AJIDI: We're as good as home, brother.

AMINI: This time, I believe we are. And while we wait for the cotton, we can finish our house.

(As the BOYS talk, BUSHCAT and LEMUR exit and re-enter with a basket of large red paper flowers.)

AJIDI: And build a bridge across the river.

AMINI: And learn more about medicine plants from Njoka the python...

AJIDI: Think I'll stick with the bridge-building.

(The BOYS exit. THE BUSHCAT, LEMUR, OSPREY, SWALLOWS, STORKS and the TSEKWES stick the flowers all over KAPOK TREE, chanting the following song as they do so.)

EVERYONE IS WELCOME

Everyone is welcome, in feathers or in fur
Anyone who wants to — can come gaze at her
Everyone is welcome — every day and every hour
To glory in the glory of the Kapok Tree in flower

Everyone is welcome, in feathers or in fur
Now she'll give soft cotton which is just like her
But what she hadn't planned on when she made the deal

(*All finish attaching the flowers and stand back.*)

A hungry old elephant in search of a meal!

(*We hear the sound of an ELEPHANT'S trumpeting from off stage. All exit except the KAPOK TREE.*)

Act 2, Scene 2 — Over To Elephant

Around the Kapok Tree. THE LONG GRASS and THORN BUSHES arrange themselves at either side of the front of the stage. NJOBVU enters and lumbers between them, swinging his trunk and sniffing right and left. He exits.

LONG GRASS: (*whispering and rustling*) Well, he may be old but he can still flatten grass.

THORN BUSHES: Luckily, he hardly touches thorns these days.

(*NJOBVU re-enters behind THE KAPOK TREE, ambles up to her and then does a double-take as he sees her flowers.*)

KAPOK TREE: (*her voice trembling*) Njobvu! What brings you to my side? Not a sudden urge to <u>uproot</u>, I hope?

NJOBVU: No, no. Your scarlet flowers, m'dear. And in a grey world they are <u>very</u> scarlet.

(*He puts his trunk up to a flower. KAPOK TREE shrinks back.*)

KAPOK TREE: But the world isn't grey, Njobvu. The rains have been. There are tender green shoots just right for eating, <u>everywhere</u>.

NJOBVU: Not to me. For an old chap like me with failing eye-sight, your flowers are about the only thing I can see or smell... or, for that matter, still chew.

(He pulls off a flower and pops it into his mouth.)

KAPOK TREE: Njobvu, Njobvu, stop that at once!

(NJOBVU munches on, picking off the flowers.)

NJOBVU: Sorry, m'dear? You were saying? I'm a bit hard of hearing, don't you know....

(KAPOK gives a faint shriek each time NJOBVU picks off a flower. TSEKWE and MRS TSEKWE enter carrying sticks for a new nest.)

TSEKWE: Now, I know how fond you are of Kapok Tree but p'rhaps we should think twice about...

MRS TSEKWE: *(shrieking)* Oh, what an <u>unnatural</u> disaster!

(She rushes over to NJOBVU, and angrily pecks his legs.)

NJOBVU: Mrs Tsekwe! What's eating you?

MRS TSEKWE: You! That's what's eating me! You!

NJOBVU: I don't think so, m'dear. I'm eating these delicious scarlet flowers. All of them... I think... Can you see any more?

(The KAPOK TREE swoons. BUSHCAT, LEMUR, OSPREY, THE STORKS AND SWALLOWS enter. ALL, including BUSHES and GRASS, register shock.)

TSEKWE: You'll never understand what you've done, Njobvu!

ALL: He never will. He's so old, he's gaga...

KAPOK TREE: *(She cranes to look at herself)* Aaaahhh!

NJOBVU: Now, I heard that. Why is she swooning?

MRS TSEKWE: Njobvu, get down here and I'll tell you.

(Slowly NJOBVU goes down on his knees.)

BUSHCAT
and LEMUR: *(aside)* Well, that's it. He'll never get up again,
                 poor old devil.

MRS TSEKWE: Njobvu, as you should know, when Kapok's flowers
                 have bloomed...

KAPOK TREE: *(recovering suddenly)* ...they explode into the softest
                 silkiest pods of cotton in the world! Ohhh! *(Looking at
                 herself, she swoons once again.)*

MRS TSEKWE: And she'd promised it to the Wingless Ones...

NJOBVU: Who?

OSPREY: The Tuskless Ones!

NJOBVU: Ah them... good boys. Dressed a wound for me once
                 with moss. But why do they want Kapok's cotton?

TSEKWE: They have a debt to pay. To their village.

NJOBVU: *(He puts his trunk up to one ear and then the other as
                 he tries to follow.)* A debt?

ALL: A debt.

OSPREY: So they were growing a field of rice to pay it with.

LEMUR: Only the Tsekwes ate the rice.

BUSHCAT: And offered them goslings instead.

NJOBVU: Quite right.

SWALLOWS: But then the wind blew.

KAPOK TREE: Raged, actually.

TSEKWE: And one of Kapok's branches fell onto the eggs.

ALL: <u>Crash</u>!

KAPOK TREE: Ohhhh!

MRS TSEKWE: So she offered her cotton instead.

NJOBVU: Should think so too.

ALL: <u>Only now you've eaten the flowers that would have turned into that cotton</u>!

NJOBVU: All right, no need to shout.

(He gets to his feet, suddenly quite together, and brushes his knees.)

NJOBVU: You think I'm an ageing old fool, don't you. Well, maybe I am, maybe I'm not. But one thing I still have is my honour. If I've dined off Kapok Tree so she can't pay her debt, then the debt passes to me. No question about it. <u>I must give something</u>!

LONG GRASS and BUSHES: *(aside)* What can an old wrinkly like him offer?

NJOBVU: And before you start asking what a wrinkly old fellow like me can offer, I'll tell you. <u>This</u>! *(He wiggles a tusk.)* It's so loose, it's no use to me.

OSPREY: And the Wingless Ones value elephant tusk above everything.

NJOBVU: Don't I know it! So, Lemur and Bushcat, if you'd be kind enough to bring me a piece of vine, we'll have the thing out in no time.

LEMUR: (*running off with BUSHCAT*) No trouble! Nothing we love more than a public extraction!

(*There is excited whispering and rustling. BUSHCAT and LEMUR run back with a long piece of 'vine'. They tie one end around NJOBVU's loose tusk. BUSHCAT, LEMUR, OSPREY, THE TSEKWES, THE STORKS and SWALLOWS get hold of the other end, as if for a tug of war.*)

NJOBVU: Are you ready? Are you steady? For the quick draw, <u>pull</u>!

(*EVERYONE pulls... cries OUCH!... and falls in a heap as the tusk comes away from NJOBVU. Lights out. ALL exit, NJOBVU carrying his tusk.*)

Act 2, Scene 3 — Over To The Ants

At the Bridge. Lights up. THE ANTS, in an army led by CHIEF PERSIST-ANT and SECOND-IN-COMMAND-ANT enter at the back of the hall and march, singing, through the audience to the stage. At the same time, the RIVER and the BRIDGE RAILS enter on the stage and arrange themselves across it as hand rails, in two parallel lines from the front to the back of the stage, with RIVER on either side. The ANTS sing the following song, to the tune of 'John Brown's Body.'

<u>MARCH OF THE ANTS</u>

White Ants marching in a column four by four
Don't bother locking it, we'll eat right through the door
Don't mind what the wood is, every wood's a meal
We're the Ants with jaws of steel..

Show us it and we will gnaw it
Grow us it and we will bore it
Need it cut and we will saw it
We're the Ants with jaws of steel!

White Ants massing like an army on the ridge
Don't bother raising it, we'll eat right through the bridge
Don't mind what the wood is, every wood's a must
We will turn it all to dust...

Show us it and we will gnaw it
Grow us it and we will bore it
Need it cut and we will saw it
We will turn it all to dust!

(The ANTS settle down to mime gnawing at the BRIDGE RAILS. DRUMMERS make grating sounds on their drums. NJOBVU lumbers in, upstage of the RIVER, carrying his tusk aloft.)

NJOBVU: Now, if my sense of direction still serves me, the Boys live on that hill over there... and a stream flows swiftly here. Oh... *(He stops and feels out the bridge space with one foot.)* How thoughtful. They've built a bridge. Much better than catching a chill, getting the old feet wet...

WHIPPER-SNAPPER: *(nudging fellow Ants)* Look, Njobvu's about to cross the bridge!

IGNOR-ANT: *(gnawing)* Who?

WHIPPER-SNAPPER: Njobvu, the old elephant.

IRRIT-ANT: So?

INTOLER-ANT: What's it to you, Whipper-Snapper?

WHIPPER-SNAPPER: We've eaten most of it away. It'll never take his weight.

MILIT-ANT: That's his look-out.

(NJOBVU steps towards the end of the BRIDGE and then between the BRIDGE RAILS. AMINI and AJIDI enter at the front of the stage. As NJOBVU stands between the BRIDGE RAILS, they begin to sway.)

AMINI: Hey! There's Njobvu.

AJIDI: He must be coming to see us.

WHIPPER-SNAPPER: Njobvu, don't cross! It's not safe!

AMINI: That's strange. He seems to be carrying a tusk...

(NJOBVU trumpets a hello to the BOYS as he continues slowly across the BRIDGE between the swaying BRIDGE RAILS.)

WHIPPER-SNAPPER: Njobvu, go back!

VIGIL-ANT: You're wasting your time!

FLAMBOY-ANT: He's as deaf as a post.

WHIPPER-SNAPPER: If we all shout together, he might hear. Come on, ready.... (squeaky) Njobvu, get off the bridge!

(NJOBVU is almost across. The BRIDGE RAILS start to fall.)

SECOND-IN-
COMMAND-ANT: Atten...shun! Bridge collapsing! Return to safe ground!

(Drumming. The ANTS scurry away from the front of the bridge and arrange themselves at either side of the stage. As the BRIDGE RAILS collapse, the swirling blue cloaks of the RIVER rise to submerge NJOBVU. The tusk flies away from him. It's picked up by members of the RIVER who pass it between them, finally concealing it beneath their cloaks.)

AMINI: Oh no! The bridge has gone!

(NJOBVU emerges from the blue swirl of the RIVER. He clambers, as if up the river bank, on the downstage side and gives himself a shake.)

AJIDI: Njobvu, are you all right?

NJOBVU: I'm all right, but my tusk... my precious tusk. Amini! Ajidi! It fell into the stream! Can you see it?

AMINI: That's a fast flowing river, Njobvu. It'll be far away by now. Anyway, what were you doing carrying a tusk?

NJOBVU: Bringing it to you. So you could pay your debt to your village and go home!

AJIDI: This was more than generous, noble Njobvu. But we don't need your tusk for that. We have Kapok Tree's cotton crop.

NJOBVU: Not any more, you don't. *(Very sadly)* I ate her flowers.

AJIDI: There'll be no cotton?

NJOBVU: No cotton and now no tusk. What a sad, bad day when I, Njobvu, have a debt and I can't pay. *(He trumpets mournfully.)*

WHIPPER-SNAPPER: Wait, wait! If you can't pay your debt, Njobvu, it is only because we weakened the bridge! So, the debt must pass to us!

(NJOBVU, AMINI and AJIDI stare at WHIPPER-SNAPPER in amazement.)

NJOBVU: I'll be jiggered. An honest White Ant!

(WHIPPER-SNAPPER scampers over to CHIEF PERSIST-ANT and falls to his knees.)

WHIPPER-SNAPPER: Permission to speak, Oh Chief Persist-Ant!

CHIEF
PERSIST-ANT: You have already spoken, without permission, Whipper-Snapper. And I have heard.

(CHIEF PERSIST-ANT steps up to NJOBVU and the BOYS.)

CHIEF PERSIST-ANT: Njobvu, you have always been careful not to tread on us and, indeed, often let us travel freely on your great feet.

NJOBVU: *(aside)* And very irritating you were too.

CHIEF PERSIST-ANT: And so, since it is true we weakened the bridge, I, Chief Persist-Ant, accept responsibility. The debt must pass to the Ants!

THE ANTS: *(shocked)* <u>To the Ants</u>?

NJOBVU, AMINI, AJIDI: *(very dubiously)* <u>To the Ants</u>?

SECOND-IN-COMMAND-ANT: You heard, <u>to the Ants</u>! So Ants, to the Council Chamber, fall in and move!

(Drumming. The ANTS fall in and march off stage, singing the last verse of their song as they go.)

White Ants massing like an army on the ridge
Seems we're in trouble since we ate right through the bridge
Nothing comes for nothing, though it chewed up very nice
We now must pay the price. PAY THE PRICE!

(Lights down. AMINI, AJIDI and NJOBVU remain where they are as the TSEKWES, BUSHCAT, LEMUR, OSPREY, SWALLOWS and STORKS join them in the dark.)

Act 2, Scene 4 — All is Lost

In and outside the Ant Hill. AMINI, AJIDI, NJOBVU, TSEKWES, BUSHCAT, LEMUR, OSPREY, SWALLOWS and STORKS walk round the stage in single file as if round the outside of an anthill. They group to one side to wait anxiously for the outcome of the ANTS' meeting. The ANTS enter and seat themselves for a council meeting.

SECOND-IN-COMMAND-ANT: Silence in the council chamber. All fall before the Great Chief Persist-Ant.

(The ANTS fall to their knees and bow heads as CHIEF PERSIST-ANT enters.)

CHIEF PERSIST-ANT: It is a long story that brings us here tonight. A story with a beginning and a middle, but no end... until we can think of something to give the Bridge-Builders so they can pay their debt. So think of something!

(The ANTS drop jaws and stare up at the CHIEF in awed silence.)

SECOND-IN-
COMMAND-ANT: You heard! Think of something!

ANTS: *(a low rumble)* Er, yes, sir, think of something!

(The ANTS drum nervously with their fingers on the ground.)

DESPOND-ANT: It's no good. There's nothing we can offer, Chief.

ARROG-ANT: We are scavengers and destroyers. And glad to be so! Despond-Ant's right. We have nothing to offer!

MILIT-ANT: And never will have!

SECOND-IN-
COMMAND-ANT: This may be true but you heard your Chief. So think again. Think harder!

ANTS: *(low muttering)* Yes, sir! Harder, sir!

(A concerted drumming of hands and fingers and 'thinking' noises like 'er, um, hmmm, think, think' etc and which quickly begins to sound like a class of children talking, muttering and whispering in a distracted way behind their teacher's back.)

AJIDI: What are they doing in there?

NJOBVU: I fear the worst.

BUSHCAT & LEMUR: You're right to. The Ants will never think of anything.

AMINI: Then all is lost.

TSEKWE: From the rice.

OSPREY: To the goslings!

STORKS &
SWALLOWS: To Kapok's cotton!

AJIDI: To an ivory tusk!

AMINI: All so generously given.

AJIDI: We might as well face it, Amini. We'll never get home this way. Come on...

(AMINI & AJIDI, NJOBVU, TSEKWES etc file out and exit.)

CHIEF PERSIST-ANT: All right, enough! Enough! This is hopeless!
Second-in-Command Ant, send a message to the Boys.
Tell them we're an army. We don't stop to think. We have no idea how to pay the debt.

(SECOND-IN-COMMAND-ANT clicks heels and salutes.)

WHIPPER-SNAPPER: Wait! I've got it!

IRRIT-ANT: Wouldn't you just!

WHIPPER-SNAPPER: Mushrooms!

WHIPPER-SNAPPER: Yes! Mushrooms! It's easy. We're carriers! We can carry mushroom spore from the hills to the fields round the Boys' village.

(The ANTS, including the CHIEF & S.I.C. are amazed at the simple brilliance of the idea and look round at each other in delight.)

ANTS: Brilliant! To the hills, it is then!

SECOND-IN-
COMMAND-ANT: To the hills, MARCH!

(DRUM ROLL. The ANTS march off. Lights out.)

Act 2, Scene 5 — And Wisdom Came Too

In the Village. The TREES and the WALLS OF THE HOUSE enter and arrange themselves as they have done before. MAMMA NOMVULA, UNCLES and the VILLAGERS enter at the back of the hall behind the audience. Some have hoes. They sing or chant as if working in the fields.

CALL:	RESPONSE:
These are good times...	These are good times...

CALL:	RESPONSE:
When the sun shines...	And the rains are on their way...

CALL:	RESPONSE:
But these are sad days, too...	Mamma Nomvula cries all day...

ALL:
Her longing never goes away.

(AMINI, AJIDI and WHIPPER-SNAPPER enter on stage.)

AMINI: And here it is! Our village. Our home! How I've ached for this day.

AJIDI: But where is everyone?

AMINI: Out in the fields. Let's call. Ahaaai! Mother? Sisters? Uncles?

AJIDI: It's us! We're home!

MAMMA
NOMVULA: Am I dreaming?

TREES and
WALLS: Not dreaming, Mamma. Not this time.

MAMMA
NOMVULA: Uncles, did you hear what I hear? Are my ears playing tricks?

AMINI & AJIDI:	Mamma! Uncles!
UNCLES:	No, you heard right, Mamma! Ajidi and Amini have returned!

(The UNCLES lead MAMMA NOMVULA and the VILLAGERS to the stage.)

FIRST UNCLE:	Go tell the Elders, the Good-Time Boys are here.

(DRUMMERS drum the rhythm 'Go tell the Elders'.)

TREES, WALLS, VILLAGERS:	*(chanting)* Go tell the Elders, the Good-Time Boys are here.
SECOND UNCLE:	What have they brought?
VILLAGERS:	Is it rice? Do they bring rice?
MAMMA NOMVULA:	Don't tell me their hands are empty.

(The ELDERS enter. AMINI and AJIDI and WHIPPER-SNAPPER each go down on one knee.)

FIRST ELDER:	Amini and Ajidi, sons of Mamma Nomvula. Why have you returned?
AJIDI:	To pay our debt, Father.
AMINI:	To be part of this village again.
SECOND ELDER:	Then where is the rice?
THIRD ELDER:	Have you not harvested yet?
AJIDI:	There is no rice, Honoured Ones.
FOURTH ELDER:	No rice?
MAMMA NOMVULA:	*(wailing)* Aaai, aaai, aaai!

FOURTH ELDER: So how will you pay your debt?

WHIPPER-SNAPPER: *(tugging at him)* Tell them, tell them!

VILLAGERS: *(whispering)* They've come empty-handed!

AMINI: Honoured Fathers, you will have to believe us.

AJIDI: On the first morning after the next rain, as far as the eye can see, from here across the fields, there will be...

WHIPPER-SNAPPER: Mushrooms!

AMINI: Mushrooms, Honoured Ones. And that is a solemn promise from the Ants who, even as we speak, are busy carrying the mushroom spore from the hills to these fields.

WHIPPER-SNAPPER: *(happily)* And it was all my idea!

(The ELDERS confer quickly and quietly.)

THIRD ELDER: Is this all you have brought?

AJIDI: Er, and a little knowledge of bridge-building...

AMINI: And of plants and herbs for medicines.

FOURTH ELDER: Anything else?

AMINI: We've learned trust, Honoured Fathers. And respect for others. And that kindness and generosity breed kindness and generosity.

AJIDI: And that hard work brings good times of its own.

(The ELDERS confer.)

MAMMA
NOMVULA: Could all this be enough to pay their debt?

FIRST ELDER: *(significant pause)* It is enough. Welcome home.

(All cry 'Welcome Home!' Drumming. MAMMA NOMVULA embraces her sons and they walk together into the HOUSE. The VILLAGERS stamp their feet and sway. There is a loud rumble of thunder from off stage. The DRUMMERS pick up rain sticks and create the sound of rain. Everyone — except for TREES & WALLS — runs to the sides of the stage as if taking shelter. WHIPPER-SNAPPER comes to the front of the stage.)

WHIPPER-SNAPPER: And so it rained. It rained and rained.

TREES, WALLS,
DRUMMERS: It rained and rained, all afternoon and all evening and most of the night.

WHIPPER-SNAPPER: I hid in the Boys' hut. At first light, I woke them and led them to the fields.

(AMINI & AJIDI come out of the HOUSE, stretch and gaze out over the audience, amazed.)

AMINI: Mushrooms as far as the eye can see!

AJIDI: The Ants have been true to their word.

WHIPPER-SNAPPER: I'd want to know why if they hadn't. Call the others. I can't wait to see their joy.

(MAMMA NOMVULA comes out of the HOUSE and stares. The VILLAGERS, UNCLES and ELDERS move forward and gaze out in wonder.)

ALL: Just as they promised. Mushrooms as far as the eye can see!

WHIPPER-SNAPPER: And now the spore is here, there will be mushrooms every time it rains!

MAMMA
NOMVULA: My sons, you have done better than I dared hope. The village will never be hungry again!

AJIDI: It's the least we owe you, Mamma.

MAMMA
NOMVULA: But what's all this?

(NJOBVU, with a red flower from the Kapok Tree, leads in the TSEKWES and the ANTS. The VILLAGERS stand back in awe.)

AMINI: These are some of the friends we've made, who
                    now become your friends. From this day we ask
                    you not to eat the kindly goose.

AJIDI: Or take ivory from the noble elephant.

AMINI: Or resent the White Ants for if they destroy they are
                    also the greatest carriers.

FIRST ELDER: Then it is not just mushrooms you have brought, Amini
                    and Ajidi. More valuable than anything — you have
                    brought wisdom. So, let us put our work aside for the
                    day and feast and sing and dance.

SECOND ELDER: The Wild Boys have become the Wise Boys.
                    And they are back!

ALL: The boys are back!

(Drumming. ALL sing or chant the following responses, as often as is desired.)

NOW OUR HEARTS SING

CALL: The boys are back   RESPONSE: Now our hearts sing
And Mamma Nomvula can
sleep at night!

CALL: Her sons are home   RESPONSE: How her heart soars
Everything here has turned
out right!

(For the final round of the singing or chanting, the whole cast and the stage management team enters, joins in and takes a bow.)

THE END

Staging

Area for performance

You can stage *The Good Time Boys* in a variety of ways. The stage directions within the playscript are written for a straightforward production in the school hall. Ideally, the hall would have a stage, platform or area at one end where the play could be performed. It would also have a door at the back of the hall and at least one entrance on to the acting area from a classroom or corridor. If you plan to stage the play in this kind of space, it's worth noting that characters in each new scene should start to enter before the characters in the previous scene have finished leaving the stage. This will give the play its essential flow and continuity. If you have access to rostra blocks, you might consider making a raised level at the back of the stage. Two stage levels are better than one! Characters sometimes approach the acting area from the back of the audience, so you would need steps up to the raised stage.

You will also need to set aside an area at one side of the stage for the Drummers, their drums and rainsticks. They should be seated so that they can see the pianist or keyboard player if you have either of these. The drummers are present throughout the play.

It's equally possible to stage the play outside or in a classroom or simple assembly room. Whichever setting you are using, it can be very effective to have the whole cast, including your stage management team, in a semi-circle around the acting area. This semi-circular area could be on an actual stage, on the floor or outside on the ground. Arrange the cast so that the parts are each grouped together. The actors with the main speaking parts should be positioned in the middle of the semi-circle, slightly in front of the other actors, so that they have easy access to the acting area.

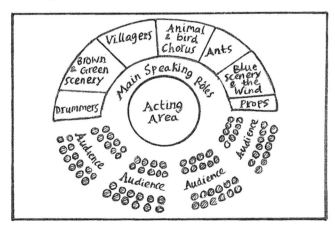

An advantage of this staging is its simplicity: props and instruments for sound effects can be placed in two large African-style baskets at the side of the acting area.

Staging

Use this general rule to help you follow the stage directions in the playscript: whenever the characters are on stage, they simply come forward into the acting area. When they are off stage, they return to their places in the semi-circle. Part of the time, many characters — particularly chorus characters — will not even need to leave the semi-circle but can perform their parts from where they sit or stand. This staging also allows the whole cast to participate in the songs and chants.

Using the Audience Area

Whichever staging you are using, there are two scenes in the play that require members of the cast to come through the audience: the ants' entrance march in Act 2, Scene 3 (Over to the Ants) and the beginning of Act 2, Scene 5 (Wisdom Came Too) when the Villagers are returning home from the fields.

In preparation for Over to the Ants, don't bring the Ants back into the semi-circle after the Interval. Let them wait at the back of the room, ready to make their big marching entrance through the middle of the audience. For Wisdom Came Too, simply get the Villagers to pick up their hoes at the end of All is Lost (Act 2, Scene 4) and walk to the back of the audience as if they were leaving their village to go to work in the fields. They can use the central or side aisles.

At the bridge

Act 2, Scene 3 (Over to the Ants) is probably the most complex of all the scenes in terms of staging and deserves special attention. The illustration shows you how the Rails can position themselves front-to-back across the stage to create the bridge, with the River to either side. Njobvu will walk forwards across the bridge from the back of the acting area.

Backdrops

There is no need for a backdrop if you stage the play in the semi-circle. If you're using a conventional stage at the end of a hall, a bare wall behind the actors will look fine. If you prefer, and have the time and resources, a stark, simple depiction of blue sky and dusty dry browny-green African bush, painted on sheeting will certainly add atmosphere and serve for the whole play.

Scenery and Props

There are five locations in the play where scenery is called for and almost all of it is provided by members of the cast. How many children you have playing each scenery part is up to you, although you will need a minimum of two in each case. The secret of successful human scenery lies largely in carefully orchestrated mime and movement. The following ideas may serve as a useful guide for movements, but please feel free to develop your own mimes with the actors. Their costumes will also help. (See page 47.) Obviously, the children will not have to hold the poses for the whole play, but only as the stage directions suggest. At other times they can kneel or sit at ease.

Trees, Thorn Bushes and Long Grass

The Trees will stand most of the time and could sway in the wind, with their arms outstretched or reaching outwards and upwards. The Thorn Bushes can wave spiky fingers in stabbing, staccato movements. The Long Grass characters can kneel with their hands held palm to palm above their heads or just below their chins, to show the grasses' flower heads.

Walls of the House

To create the house, the children will arrange themselves in a small circle, facing inwards with their arms raised to touch hands at the apex of the roof. They should all use the same arm (left or right) to put their hand behind their ear when the stage directions demand it.

Lapping Water, River, Rushes and Wind

River and Lapping Water will spend most of their time crouching down, waving their pieces of swirly material to create the effect of water. In contrast, the Rushes will stand straight and upright with their arms by their sides, swaying from time to time. The Wind will have the most dramatic movements, whirling wildly across the stage.

Around the Kapok Tree

If you are using the row of rostra blocks at the back of the stage you could position the tree just in front of them. The chorus of animals and birds could stand on the blocks to reach her branches. If you don't have rostra blocks and are staging the scene on the flat, then animals and birds will simply reach up to the tree's branches.

Scenery and Props

Have a props table or African-style basket close to the stage entrance or at the edge of your acting area, overseen by your props person. The cast can collect their props before each scene.

Act 1, Scene 1
Dice for Amini and Ajidi
Axe for Amini
Hoe and seeds for Ajidi
Act 1, Scene 2
As Scene 1
Bow and arrow for Amini
Act 1, Scene 3
Bow and arrow for Amini
Act 1, Scene 4
Nest for Mrs Tsekewe
Act 2, Scene 1
Bow and arrow for Amini
Red paper flowers for the tree
Act 2, Scene 2
A basket
10-12 paper flowers
Vine
Act 2, Scene 5
Hoes for villagers
Red paper flower for Njobvu

Some of these props are easy to find. For instance, Amini can have a plastic toy bow and arrow and the Tsekwe's nest could be a wicker dog basket with a cushion inside it. Some of the props will need to be made. Here are some ideas:

An axe
To make an axe, find a long cardboard tube from a roll of wrapping paper and make a slit at one end. Cut the blade out of strong cardboard and glue it to the slit. Finish it with a coat of paint.

Hoes
If you can't find a child's toy garden hoe, you can easily improvise with simple wooden poles or broom handles.

Seeds
The seeds could be a small sack of dry rice tied with string.

Flowers
To make the red paper flowers for the Kapok tree, you will need some red tissue paper or crepe. Cut out a large circle (about 20 cm across) and one slightly smaller. Place the smaller circle on top of the larger one. Fold them into a semi-circle and then a quarter circle. Staple the pointed end. Open the flower up and arrange the petals. You can use double-sided tape to make the flowers stick to the tree.

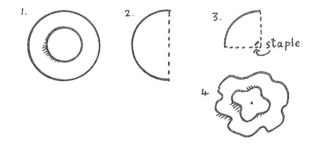

Vine
The vine could be a simple piece of natural coloured twine with paper leaves attached.

Lighting

There is no special lighting needed and lighting directions in the playscript are kept to the minimum: "lights down" or "lights up". If you have stage lights available, then you can follow these directions and add further lighting effects for heightened drama.

For example, you can create lightning flashes for the storm in Act 1, Scene 4 (Natural Disaster). In Act 2, Scene 4 (All is Lost), you could make the Ants' council chamber dark and shadowy with a spotlight on the Chief Persist-Ant. If you have no stage lighting, it will be perfectly adequate to turn ceiling lights on and off where the script requires it.

Casting and Auditions

When it comes to casting the play, you need to consider the different demands of the various roles. In this particular play there isn't the usual division between big speaking parts and smaller non-speaking parts. You could explain to the children that parts such as Lapping Water and Wind call for a lot of mime and movement, if not speech.

A good way to start the audition process would be to hold a pre-casting workshop for all the children interested in being involved in some way. Tell them the story of the play and describe the characters, using the notes on pages 42–43 as a guide. Talk about the functions of other roles, such as Lapping Water, Wind, other scenery parts and the Drummers. Make the point that there are also many important jobs to be done behind the scenes. Emphasise that co-ordinated teamwork both on and off the stage will be vital to the success of the production. This doesn't mean that there won't be plenty of fun involved too and the result will certainly be satisfying!

Casting and Auditions

The Auditions

Before you start your auditioning exercises, you could set the mood with recordings of African music. Talk to the children about the role of drumming in Africa, how drums were used to send messages and tell stories.

Let everybody try for a part if they wish to do so. As mime, movement and rhythm are so important in this play, you will be looking for dancers and drummers, as well as actors. They will all be important to the success of the play! The following exercises will help you to identify children to take on these various roles.

* Play recordings of African-style music for the children to dance to. The villagers, Mamma Nomvula, the Uncles, Amini and Ajidi need to be good stampers and dancers. The Kapok tree must be able to move beautifully.

* Ask the children to make up drumming rhythms for different moods — news of war, news of victory, a storm approaching, etc. Give them some words to set to drumming, such as "Nothing but a good time" and "Call the boys" (Act 1, Scene 1). Remember — no sticks are allowed, just hands!

* Ask the children to mime the movement of "lapping water" or "trees wilting in the sun". You could give them some ideas about how to do this. How would they make Lapping Water's "husha husha husha" noise? What movements would they use to suggest wilting in the sun or the spikiness of thorn trees? How would they show you a "gale force wind"?

* Divide the children into groups and ask them to imitate the movement of different animals that appear in the play, such as waddling geese, marching ants, lumbering elephants.

* Divide the children into groups of four and ask them to improvise the moment in Act 1, Scene 3 (Over to the Geese) when Ajidi and Amini discover the Tsekwes eating rice.

* Divide the children into groups of five or six to improvise the moment in Act 1, Scene 4 when the Kapok Tree's branch falls off.

Read through

The next step will be to organise the "read-through". Copy the play so that everyone can have a sight of it. Let a number of different children have a go at the various parts before you make your final decision. Fortunately, it is possible to create parts for everyone who wants one, by expanding the numbers of Villagers, Trees, Grasses, Lapping Water and so on. Once the casting is done, the all-important stage management jobs can be allocated to those children who prefer not to appear on stage, but who want an important role in the production.

The Main Characters

Amini
More thoughtful and sensitive at first, by the end he has developed practical strength.

Ajidi
Manipulative to start with, he becomes more sensitive and down to earth.

Njobvu the elephant
Once wise and great — now growing vulnerable with age.

Tsekwe and Mrs Tsekwe
The 'silly geese' — endearingly dependent on each other.

The Kapok Tree
Beautiful, vain and sociable.

Mamma Nomvula

A traditional 'mother figure' with conflicting emotions about her sons' behaviour.

The Animal/Bird Chorus

Fun commentators on the action, straight out of the African bush.

The Ants

A disorderly regiment, they are the comic turn of the play, with young Whipper-Snapper, the eager hero.

The Villagers, Uncles and Elders

The 'chorus', demonstrating the social structure of an African village of the time.

The Wind

A force of nature beyond any control.

The Stage Management Team

This should be composed of six or seven responsible and capable children who will be involved in your production from the start. Some of the jobs may need some adult supervision but the more responsibility given to the team, the more involved they will feel.

Props Person
To ensure all props are displayed on the props table (or in the props basket) before each performance and to make sure they are returned afterwards.

Scenery Supervisors
Two children to support the scenery parts and ensure they're in the right place at the right time as well as moving any physical scenery on and off stage.

Sound Effects
One member of the team could be in charge of creating the effects. He or she will need a playscript marked with all sound effect cues.

Lighting
Another member of the team could be responsible for turning lights on and off. He/she will also need a script marked with lighting cues. If you use more complex lighting, he/she could assist the adult in charge.

Prompter
The prompter should be seated near the edge of the stage or in the wings with a script and ready to help with forgotten lines.

Front of House
Two or three members dressed as Villagers to show the audience to their seats and hand out programmes.

Directors Assistant
Someone there, at your side, at all times, to make notes, take messages, make lists and generally act as your right-hand man or woman.

Rehearsal Schedule

Work out a rehearsal schedule as soon as the play is cast. A good method is to rehearse the play in sections, calling only those needed for that section to attend. You may also want to rehearse your scenery parts, chorus parts and those with main speaking roles separately to start with. You will probably need to plan for a run-through with everything in place including lighting and sound effects before the dress rehearsal.

Costume

Female Roles

Mamma Nomvula and village women

Mamma Nomvula, the women in the village and any girls who are drummers should all wear bright pieces of material tied at their waist with a brightly coloured tee-shirt. Alternatively, they could wear longer pieces of material, tied under their arms like beach wraps. One way of creating an African look would be to tie-dye sheets to use as sarong material. The sarongs need to wrap one and a half times around the child to stop them flapping open. You can also use safety pins to fix them firmly into position. The girls can also wear traditional African-style head dresses, made from simple pieces of cloth as shown. They can wear simple sandals or go barefoot.

The Kapok Tree

The Kapok Tree can wear a green and red sarong to suggest her leaves and flowers. Use a long-sleeved top so that her branches can be fixed to her arms. You may use real twigs for the branches. Alternatively, make branches using cardboard tubes from wrapping paper rolls. These should be light enough to attach to the costume with strips of strong masking tape. Make slits in the tube and use glue to attach cardboard 'twigs'. Decorate with paper leaves.

Male Roles

The men of the village and boys who are drummers can wear long shifts made by attaching two rectangles of cloth at the shoulders. You could tie-dye sheets to make these. They can also wear beads or necklaces of painted pasta quills or shells. Amini and Ajidi could wear short shifts or loin cloths. They can all wear simple sandals or go barefoot.

Join the material here

Costume

Njobvu

His basic costume can be a grey tracksuit. Make a headband from a piece of card measuring 60 cm by 4 cm wide. Fit it to the child's head and staple the ends. Huge grey ears can be made from card and stapled to the headband. Tusks can be cut out of thick white card. Use staples or tape to attach them to the side of the headband, remembering that one tusk will need to be easily removable for Act 2, Scene 2. To make a trunk, you will need an adult's grey sock. Draw a pair of black nostrils at the foot end with felt pen. Slip the sock over the child's arm and under the tracksuit sleeve.

Njobvu

Male Ants

The Chief can be modelled on an African warrior. He can wear a shift with a 'leopard-skin' cloak and headband, a shield and face paints. To create your own leopard skin, use a thick marker pen to make black spots on any beige or brown material. The cloak should be very simple and irregular in shape. The headband can be made from the same material and tied at the back of the actor's head. Attach antennae to the headband and use them to depict huge ant eyes. The shield can be cut out of cardboard and painted light brown. Attach a small strap at the back so it can easily be carried. The Second-in-Command can be dressed as the unisex ants (see below), but he might be distinguished by a face-paint moustache and a short stick tucked under his arm. Make a simple headband like Njobvu's for his antennae.

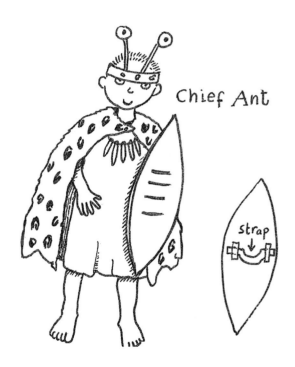

Chief Ant

strap

Unisex Parts

The Army of Ants

Try to get as close as you can to fatigues. If you stick to colours such as khaki, beige, green and brown and use chino style trousers you should create the right effect. Football boots would add to the effect and make a terrific noise! Make them headbands with exaggeratedly long antennae.

Costume

Birds
As far as possible, choose clothing colours appropriate to each bird. They can wear leggings and leotards or tops. The Tsekwes could be grey and white with a yellow beak, the Storks white with a red beak, and so on. Make their beaks quite simply from strips of thin card 65 cm long and 10 cm wide, as shown.

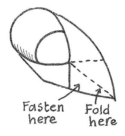 

Fasten here   Fold here

Bushcat (serval) and Lemur
Use leggings and leotards for the basic costume. Lemur's headband could show his huge round eyes. He should be dressed in grey with a grey and white striped tail. Bushcat will need a brown costume with a stripy brown tail. You can make the tails out of old stockings stuffed with rags. Paint on the stripes and attach them to the child's leggings.

Scenery parts

Use a basic costume of tights or leggings and leotards or tops for these parts.

The Trees, Thorn Bushes and Grasses
The plant parts can wear shades of green, beige, grey and brown. The Trees can have green paper leaves tacked-on to their costumes. The Thorn Bushes could have spiky wristbands, ankle bands and necklaces. You could make these from strips of material or crepe paper cut into pointy zigzags. Attach long, thin strands of pale green and yellow crepe or material to the Long Grasses' costumes and use darker green strands for the Rushes. (see p38 for illustration.)

Lapping Water and River
The parts of Lapping Water and the River can easily be played by the same cast members. They should wear different shades of blue and white with swirly pieces of blue or green material that they can wave about. These could be attached to the end of a sleeve so they don't get mislaid. The Wind's costume can be identical, but in white or grey. (See page 38 for illustration.)

Walls of house

House Walls
The House Walls can be dressed in yellow with grass skirts made of rafia or crepe paper to create the impression of straw. Use a piece of elastic to create the waistband and knot the rafia or strips of paper to it.

The Bridge Rails
The Bridge Rails will need all-over woody-brown costumes.

Music

If you haven't staged musicals or concerts before, the following ideas may help you with the play's musical background.

The play includes several chants and one song. The 'March of the Ants' is easy to perform as the lyric is written to the tune of 'John Brown's Body'. The remaining songs can be recited or chanted to the accompaniment of stamping, clapping, drumming and dancing. Keep the beat simple and regular; decide which words are the most important to stress, then have the percussion instruments beat out a rhythm based on those words.

Keep the instrumental backing simple: percussion, wind instruments and perhaps some guitars or a keyboard are ample. It's easy to make your own percussion. For a shaker, pour some dried lentils, beans or peas into a plastic pot with a lid. To make drums, cover the tops of containers such as cardboard tubes, coffee or biscuit tins with circles of polythene cut from plastic shopping bags. Pull them tightly across the opening and fasten them with elastic bands. For a rainstick, push a spiral of crushed wire netting into a cardboard tube, pour in a handful of dried peas or rice and seal the open end. Experiment!

The opening lines of Act 2, Scene 5 use a technique known as 'call and response'. A line recited or sung by one part of the cast is answered by another line from the rest. Concentrate first on getting the children to stress the key words and establish a rhythm for the lines. You could then add some drums for emphasis.

Rainsticks are called for in the last scene. The Wind could also use these, bringing them on stage in the storm scene in Act 1, Scene 4. The Villagers could bring on African-style percussion instruments and use them in Act 1, Scene 1 and the final scene. But at all times, and in all events, keep your drummers drumming.

If you want to include more singing, ask a musical member of staff, friend, or parent to compose some tunes with an African beat for the chants. If you are musical, try composing some tunes yourself or see what the children can come up with. Remember that with African music, one tune or theme is often repeated with harmonies, over and over again.

Sound Effects

If you have a loud speaker system available, you might like to use sound effect tapes (the BBC do a whole range). Otherwise, the sounds can be made by the cast themselves or your Sound Effects person.

Birds and cicadas = for the birds, a water-whistle (available from toy shops). If you're not using a sound cassette, forget about the cicadas!

Geese honking = a party-pack horn or old-fashioned bicycle horn.

Thunder = a wobble-board or metal thunder sheet.

Njobvu's trumpet = blow through a rolled up cardboard fog horn.

Rain = try rainsticks.
